To City Girl, Mei, and her parents, Richard and Gisela
—MS

To Lucy and Chaz
—CC

Clarion Books
a Houghton Mifflin Company imprint
215 Park Avenue South, New York, NY 10003
Text copyright © 2007 by Marilyn Singer
Illustrations copyright © 2007 by Carll Cneut

The illustrations were executed in acrylics mixed with dry pastels and oil pastels.
The text was set in 20-point Providence Alt-Medium.

www.clarionbooks.com

Printed in Singapore

Library of Congress Cataloging-in-Publication Data

Singer, Marilyn.
City lullaby / by Marilyn Singer ; illustrated by Carll Cneut.
p. cm.
Summary: A baby in a stroller sleeps listening to loud city noises, from ten horns
beeping to two motorbikes roaring, until awakened by the soft chirp of one sparrow.
ISBN: 978-0-618-60703-7
[1. City and town life—Fiction. 2. Noise—Fiction. 3. Babies—Fiction.
4. Counting. 5. Stories in rhyme.] I. Title.
PZ8.3.S6154 Ci 2007
[E] 22
2006100055

ISBN-13: 978-0-618-60703-7   ISBN-10: 0-618-60703-X

TWP 10 9 8 7 6 5 4 3 2 1

CiTy Lullaby

by Marilyn Singer   Illustrated by Carll Cneut

Clarion Books * New York

Traffic jam, **10** horns beeping.
In the stroller, Baby's sleeping.

Ice cream truck jing-a-linging.
9 annoying cell phones ringing.
Nine phones ringing, ten horns beeping.
In the stroller, Baby's sleeping.

Air brakes hiss. Is that truck parking?
8 excited dogs start barking.

Garbage truck, wheezing, mashing!
7 trash cans clanging, bashing.
Seven cans bashing, eight dogs barking.
Nine phones ringing, ten horns beeping.
In the stroller, Baby's sleeping.

Ack-ack-ack, jackhammer drilling.
6 car alarms whooping, shrilling.

Thrum-throb-whirr, helicopter hovers.
5 cabs rattle manhole covers.
Five cabs rattling, six alarms shrilling,
Seven cans bashing, eight dogs barking,
Nine phones ringing, ten horns beeping.
In the stroller, Baby's sleeping.

Kids swinging hard, yelling, pumping.
4 b-ball players thump-thump-thumping.

Down below, subways rumbling.
Up the street, three buses grumbling.
3 buses grumbling, four players thumping,
Five cabs rattling, six alarms shrilling,
Seven cans bashing, eight dogs barking,
Nine phones ringing, ten horns beeping.
In the stroller, Baby's sleeping.

Police car siren whining, howling.
2 motorbikes revving, roaring, growling.
Windows shake and lampposts jitter.

Then **1** bird begins to twitter.

2 bikes growling,

3 buses grumbling,

4 players thumping,

5 cabs rattling,

6 alarms shrilling,

7 cans bashing,

8 dogs barking,

9 phones ringing,

10 horns beeping.

In the stroller, Baby kept sleeping.
But one small bird, for goodness sake,
Chirpity-chirps,
Tweet!

. . . and Baby's awake!